THE STORY OF PETER LITTLE BEAR

A Lamprey River Adventure

David Allan and Leslie Hamilton
Illustrations by David Allan and Amy Daskal

PublishingWorks
Exeter, New Hampshire
2005

Published by

PublishingWorks
4 Franklin Street
Exeter, New Hampshire 03833

800/333-9883 www.publishingworks.com

Distributed to the trade by Enfield Distribution

ISBN: 1-933002-04-2

The story about "How Dog People Came to Live with Human People" is a genuine Abenaki legend. You can read it and other stories like it in Joseph Bruchac's book, *Dog People: Native Dog Stories* (Golden, CO: Fulcrum Publishers, September 1995).

Oversight and funding for this book were provided by the Lamprey River Advisory Committee, with financial assistance from the Lee Historical Society and the Lee Conservation Commission.

CONTENTS

AUTHOR'S NOTE

This story is a work of fiction. While some locations, landmarks, and events are real, the characters, their conversations, and their actions are not.

The stone pestle, the cave called Peter's Oven, and the Battle at Wheelwright's Pond are real, and served as David Allan's inspiration for the original version of this story.

The stone pestle is on display at the Lee Historical Society in Lee, New Hampshire.

Peter's Oven is on the north side of George Bennett Road, about one-eighth of a mile east of Route 125 in Lee, New Hampshire.

Wheelwright's Pond is at the intersection of Route 125 and Steppingstones Road in Lee, New Hampshire.

Boldface words in the text are defined or discussed in the Glossary at the end of this book.

LEE, NEW HAMPSHIRE

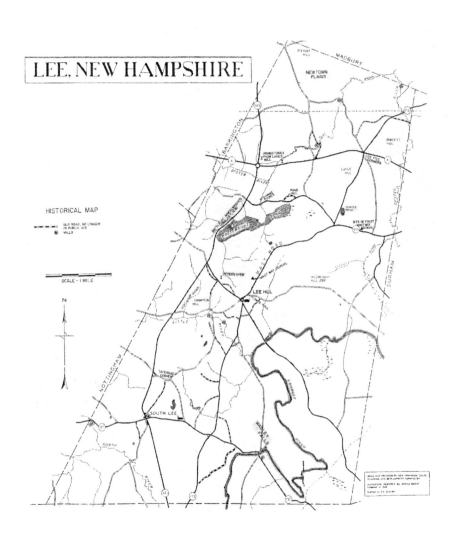

HISTORICAL MAP

- - - OLD ROAD, NO LONGER IN PUBLIC USE
- MILLS

SCALE - 1 MILE

N

1

THE PENTUCKET TRAIL, 1682

"Peter Little Bear! Hurry up! You're falling behind again!"

Little Bear scowled, groaned, and picked up his pace to join his mother, Morning Star, at the end of the line. He knew that when she used his full name, she meant business.

It had been a long winter for his family, camped high in the **Ossipee Mountains**. Now that it was springtime, the families of the **Washucke** clan traveled down from the mountains, leaving their hunting camps behind them. They walked for days to gather at their warm-weather camp near the **Lamprey River**. Little Bear's family had followed the narrow **Newichawannok Trail** until it joined with the great **Pentucket Trail**. Each time another family emerged from the woods and joined the group, they were greeted with warm hugs and laughter. As the clan hiked past familiar landmarks, they knew they were getting closer to their spring camp. Everyone was smiling with excitement as they made their way, single file, down the trail.

Everyone except Little Bear.

"You're carrying a heavy load this year, aren't you?" said Morning Star, ruffling his shiny black hair. "Don't worry. We will stop for a rest soon."

Each member of every family carried supplies needed to set up camp. Even the smallest child carried something. This year, Peter Little Bear, son of Swift Wolf and Morning Star, carried the stone **pestle**. The pestle belonged to the whole clan. It was made from a special kind of rock called **schist**. It was about two feet long and had been smoothed all over and then rounded at each end. The Washucke women used the pestle to grind **maize**, nuts, and other plants into flour or meal. Sometimes the pestle was used to grind dried meat or fish into a powder to make a food called **pemmican**. At other times, it was used to grind herbs, seeds, or other ingredients to make medicine. It was the clan's largest pestle, and they used it almost every day.

Little Bear knew he should feel proud to be carrying such a precious object. His father, Swift Wolf, was the clan's **sachem**, or leader, and carrying the pestle was a great honor for an eight-year-old boy. But the pestle was very heavy and hard to carry. Even wrapped in its deerskin pouch, the rock dug into Little Bear's back with every step. As he plodded wearily down the trail, he envied his little sister, White Fawn, who skipped along with a lightweight bundle of baskets and carved wooden spoons. The family's two dogs, Digger and Smells Bad, trotted beside her, their tongues hanging out and their tails in the air.

Finally the group stopped to rest. Little Bear felt grouchy and didn't want to sit with the others, who were laughing and telling stories. Scowling to himself, he wandered into the woods to be alone. With a loud groan, he swung the pouch off his back and set it down with a thud, next to a fallen log. He stretched his arms and back, rubbing the sore spots. A gray squirrel chattered noisily at him from a nearby tree, and two chipmunks chased each other through the tangle of bushes and brush. Little Bear chased after them until they disappeared inside a hollow log. He was about to peek into the hollow when he noticed a small, round pond that had formed in a **kettle hole**. The water was clean and clear and mostly covered with lily pads and green algae. The pond was surrounded by lush, green ferns, and insects buzzed over its surface. Little Bear spotted a few frogs hopping in and out along the water's edge.

Slowly and quietly, he crept up on the frogs and then pounced, arms outstretched and hands together. The frogs leaped away just in the nick of time, and Little Bear lost his footing and slid right into the water with a splash. The pond exploded with activity as dozens of frogs dove for safety. Little Bear was standing knee deep in pond water when he heard his mother calling from the trail.

"Peter Little Bear! Hurry! We're on our way!"

His mother's voice sounded far away, and Little Bear couldn't see her through the dense forest. He quickly waded out of the water and scampered through the underbrush, following the sound of her voice. When he found her, the group had already started moving. He took his usual place at the end of the line, relieved that Morning Star hadn't noticed he was dripping wet. It was only after they had crossed a small river and hiked for quite a distance up a steep hillside of towering pines, oaks, and maples that he suddenly remembered the pestle.

He grabbed at his back, just to check, but the pestle wasn't there. His heart began to pound, and he shivered with fear and dread. He had left the pestle behind! He knew the entire clan would be angry with him, but he was afraid to tell anyone, and he was afraid to go back and look for it. They were moving quickly toward the evening's campsite, and he knew he could easily get lost in the woods.

"Maybe someone else picked it up," he thought to himself, hopefully.

The group had traveled about a mile farther before he found the courage to tell his mother.

"Oh, Little Bear, how could you?" she scolded him. "You know how important the pestle is!"

Morning Star called to the others to stop. As with all important decisions, the clan talked together about what to do. Finally, with a stern look at his son, Swift Wolf said, "I have walked this trail many times and I know it very well. If all are agreed, Peter Little Bear and I will go back and look for the pestle. We will meet you later at the campsite."

The elders approved of the plan. His face dark

with anger, Swift Wolf turned and headed back into the forest, moving briskly down the trail. Feeling heavy with shame, Little Bear ran along behind him, trying to keep up with his father's long strides. They traveled in silence until the anger faded from Swift Wolf's face, and his pace slowed for his son.

"Little Bear," he said, "do you understand why losing the pestle is such a serious mistake?"

"Because it's important," Little Bear mumbled sadly.

"That's true," said Swift Wolf. "We use it to make many of our foods. It is one of our clan's most valuable tools and we use it almost every day."

"Can't we just make another one?" his son asked.

"It would be very hard to make a new pestle," Swift Wolf answered. "It is made from a special kind of stone that we only find high in the great **White Mountains**. It takes many days to get there, and finding just the right stone is difficult. Any other kind of stone will crack or split when we try to shape it. We bring the stone back to camp, and our toolmakers must smooth it and round the ends to make the right shape. That takes many days as well."

Finally they reached the spot where the group had stopped to rest. Little Bear found his frog pond right away, but the forest looked different in the afternoon light. He couldn't find the fallen log where he had left the pestle. He and Swift Wolf searched in wider and wider circles, fanning out from the pond in all directions.

"Where is it?" Little Bear thought as he searched. "Why can't I find it?"

They used their hands to move aside the thick cover of ferns and underbrush, but the sun began to set, and the light grew too dim to search anymore. With a sigh, Swift Wolf said they had to turn back. Father and son hiked quietly back up the trail as the forest grew dark and the first stars appeared in the night sky. Finally, a glimpse of the campfire guided them to where the clan had gathered. Everyone grew silent as the sachem and his son approached.

"Peter Little Bear and I could not find the pestle," Swift Wolf told them. "We searched for a long time, but it was not there. Perhaps the Great Spirit has taken it back and wants us to make a new one. We will talk about this tomorrow, after we have set up our camp."

Little Bear sat next to his father, staring miserably into the campfire. Morning Star brought over some food, but Little Bear had no appetite. He was glad when the flames finally died down to embers and everyone wandered off to sleep.

2

THE CAMPSITE BY THE LAMPREY RIVER

The next morning dawned sunny and warm as the clan set up their springtime camp. The camp was called **Washucke**, or "place on the hill," and the families who gathered there took their clan name from it. Every spring, as far back as anyone could remember, the clan returned to this place to grow crops, gather wild plants, and catch the salmon, shad, and other fish that swam up the Lamprey River to **spawn.** The soil at Washucke was fertile and perfect for growing crops. The forest was filled with animals to hunt and wild plants to eat or use for medicine. Little Bear loved Washucke because he got to swim and play in the river, but even the work was fun—fishing, trapping animals, or chasing crows out of the garden.

The camp was on a hill just east of a waterfall. Long ago, the men had burned and cleared a large stretch of level ground, and the clan had built their shelters, called **wigwams**, there. Most of the wigwam frames from past years were still usable, and only needed to be covered with sheets of birch bark or woven cattail mats. But some new frames had to be built. The men went into the forest and cut many tall, thin saplings of hickory, elm, or basswood. They used stone axes as well as iron axes the tribe had received in trade from the white settlers nearby. The trees they chose were strong and flexible when they were green, and the wood dried without cracking or splintering.

Everyone helped trim off the branches and carry the wood back to the campsite. Even White Fawn carried her share of small sticks, and Digger and Smells Bad each dragged a bushy branch in their mouths. Of course, when they reached the campsite, the dogs settled down in the shade of a tree and chewed their sticks into splinters.

To make a wigwam, the men sharpened the bottom of each sapling and pounded the poles into the ground in a big circle. They bent the poles over and used **sinew** to lash the tops together. The men and women lashed smaller saplings around the outer poles for strength until the structure looked like a big overturned bowl. Then the women covered the framework with sheets of birch bark or layers of tightly woven mats made from cattail reeds that would keep out wind and rain. A hole was left at the top of each wigwam to let out smoke from fires built inside. The doorways faced east, toward the rising sun, and were covered with birch bark or another cattail mat to keep mosquitoes out.

By the time the wigwams were built, it was almost midday and the sun was high in the sky. Swift Wolf gathered the clan around him, and they talked about the lost pestle. "It was our family who lost the pestle, so our family will replace it," he said. "If all agree, Morning Star's brother, Joseph Running Deer, will make the long journey to the mountains to find a proper stone. When he returns, my father, Eagle Wind, will shape the stone into a new pestle."

The elders nodded in agreement. Joseph Running Deer was one of the clan's strongest runners and a good toolmaker as well. He gathered some supplies, a small sack of cornmeal, and some dried meat. Then he said goodbye to his family, picked up his bow and quiver of arrows, and set off down the trail. Smells Bad followed at his heels, sniffing the air and wagging his tail with excitement. Little Bear wished that he could go with them. He hoped his uncle would return safely and soon.

While the women and girls set up the rest of the campsite, the men of the clan headed down the hill toward the Lamprey River to build a **fishing weir**. Little Bear and his friends, Smoke Catcher and Sleepy Eyes, followed after them. As the men decided where to build the structure, the boys played a game to see who could throw a rock all the way across the river. Smoke Catcher and Sleepy Eyes were younger and smaller than Little Bear, and their rocks only made it halfway across.

"Peter Little Bear, you're bigger than we are," complained Sleepy Eyes. "You should step back from the water to make it a little harder."

"Yes," added Smoke Catcher, laughing. "Step *way, way* back and close your eyes!"

Little Bear shrugged and took a few steps back. He chose a river rock about the size of an acorn, closed his eyes, and threw the rock as hard as he could.

"Ayyyy!" His rock hit Swift Wolf squarely in the back. "Hey, you boys! Come over here and make yourselves useful." His father gave him a stern look, but Little Bear could tell he wasn't angry. Swift Wolf handed him a stone with a very sharp edge. "Peter Little Bear, take this knife and go cut as many willow branches as you can. We need them long and thin. Get your friends to help you." He paused and then added, "And don't lose the knife."

The men decided to build the weir at a point below the falls where the water was fairly shallow. In recent years, they had been forced to move the weir farther from the falls, away from the **sawmill** built by the white settlers who had come to the area. Once they found a good spot, they set to work cutting down

The Weir

strong, slender saplings. Then they trimmed off the branches and cut the poles into lengths about six feet long. They drove the poles into the streambed, evenly spacing them from one side of the river to the other, leaving a gap in the center. Meanwhile, the boys had made a pile of willow branches nearby. The men wove the flexible branches in and out of the upright poles to form two strong woven walls that spanned the width of the river.

As the fish struggled their way upstream to spawn, the weir would serve as a barrier that confused the fish and channeled them into the opening in the center. As they swam by, the men would spear them or scoop them up with **dip nets** made from woven cattail leaves or other fibers.

Last, the men placed large boulders along the bottom of the weir to strengthen it and hold it in place. It was a very hard job. When it was done, everyone was wet, tired, and ready to return to camp. With Swift Wolf leading the way, the weary group headed toward the welcome smell of campfires and cooking food.

"Wait!" Little Bear suddenly shouted. He turned around and raced back to the weir as fast as he could. He dug around under a large rock for a moment and then came running back. "Your knife!" he said, smiling, as he placed the sharpened tool in his father's hand.

Swift Wolf patted his son on the back as they turned again toward camp. "I know you didn't mean to lose the pestle, Little Bear," he said. "Thank you for remembering my knife today."

3

STORIES AROUND THE CAMPFIRE

Peter Little Bear's grandfather, Eagle Wind, was the oldest member of the clan and their most experienced toolmaker. He had made hundreds of blades, arrowheads, and spearheads in his lifetime. He was very wise in the ways of the world and was also a wonderful storyteller. Many evenings, the clan gathered around the campfire and listened to his stories about days of long ago and about the mighty **Gluskabe.**

This night, Eagle Wind talked about the time when his father and grandfather lived. In those days, before the white men came, the Indian people were great in number, and there were many powerful tribes. Wherever water ran fresh and clean, and fish and game were plentiful, the Indians built wigwams, grew crops, and lived in harmony with the land. Then one day, huge boats with billowing sails appeared, carrying hundreds of pale-skinned people from across the Great Water.

"When we first saw them," said Eagle Wind, "we thought the boats were floating islands and the white sails were clouds."

The new settlers spoke a strange language. Instead of wigwams, they built large wooden structures for their dwellings. They wore odd-looking homespun clothing made from densely woven fibers. Eagle Wind said that the Indians welcomed the newcomers to their land and taught them how to hunt and fish, and what plants were good to eat and which were poisonous.

Eagle Wind's voice grew solemn. "But then the **Great Illness** came to our people and most of us got

very sick. There was horrible suffering everywhere, and we couldn't escape the grasp of this evil spirit. Our **powwaws** tried every kind of magic and medicine they knew, but nothing could stop the terrible sickness, and almost all of our people died—men and women, young and old. In three years, where great Indian villages once stood, there was now empty land. Wigwams stood empty and collapsed. Fishing weirs rotted and washed away downstream. Racks for drying fish and tanning animal skins blew away in the wind. From the land of the Micmacs in the north to the Mahicans in the south, all was desolate and empty."

The fire snapped and crackled in the darkness. Everyone sat in silence, subdued by the sad story of their ancestors. Then White Fawn asked, "But Grandfather, if everyone died, how are *we* here?"

The group laughed as Eagle Wind explained, "My father and mother were some of the lucky ones, Granddaughter. A small number of us survived and had children, and their children had children, and on and on until now. And today, we have you!"

White Fawn snuggled closer to Morning Star and hugged her favorite cornhusk doll to her chest.

Little Bear piped up. "Grandfather, will you tell us a story about the great Gluskabe? Please? Those stories are the best!" He looked around at the large circle of faces glowing in the firelight and saw people nodding their heads and smiling.

The old man's wrinkled face softened with a smile. He settled back as the children and elders leaned forward, eager to hear every word. Eagle Wind closed his eyes and began.

"Here we are, gathered around this fire, beneath these beautiful stars and black sky. We are the Washucke clan, part of the great **Abenaki** nation. We are the People of the Dawn. But who knows how we really came to be? I will tell you about the time when Gluskabe spoke with the animal people, just before he made the first human people.

Eagle Wind paused a moment and puffed on his clay pipe filled with sweet-smelling tobacco. Little Bear slapped at a few mosquitoes while he waited, and leaned over to poke his friend Sleepy Eyes, who was nodding off and had begun to snore.

"Long, long ago," Eagle Wind continued, "the Great Spirit made the World and all the plants and animals. When he was finished, he stood up, brushed the dirt and dust from his hands, and walked away. That dirt and dust from the Great Spirit's hands gathered itself together and formed Gluskabe, the helper to the Great Spirit.

"One day, Gluskabe was walking through the forest and thought, 'It is time to make human beings, but I wonder how the animals will treat them? I'd better find out!' So he called all the animals to come together, and they did, from the very smallest to the very tallest. Then he said, 'My friends, I am about to make some new beings, but I want to know how you will treat them. I want each one of you to come to me. I will whisper the name of the beings in your ear and you will tell me what you will do.'

"Back in ancient times," said Eagle Wind, "animals used to be much bigger than they are now. Bear was the very biggest of the animals, as tall as the trees, with long, sharp teeth and powerful claws. He proudly came forward first.

"Gluskabe whispered the Abenaki word for human beings in Bear's ear. '*Alnobak!*'

"Bear let out a frightening roar that shook the earth and he growled, 'I will tear them limb from limb! I will swallow them up!'

"'Ayy!' said Gluskabe. 'Bear, you are way too fierce!' He gently stroked Bear's black fur and Bear became much smaller. 'Now you can't be so dangerous to humans. Run away into the forest.'

"Then Moose came forward. In the old days, Moose was almost as big as Bear, and had sharp antlers as big as tree limbs.

"Gluskabe whispered the name for human beings in Moose's ear. '*Alnobak!*'

"Moose reared up on his hind legs and roared, 'I will toss them into the air with my antlers and then trample them under my hooves!'

"Gluskabe pushed on Moose's nose. Moose's nose bent under and he grew smaller until he was the size that he is today. 'Now you will not hurt the human beings. Run away into the forest.'

"Squirrel was next to come forward. In those days, Squirrel was very big and was the fiercest and meanest of all the animals.

"'*Alnobak!*' Gluskabe whispered in his ear.

"Squirrel let out a thunderous shriek and screamed, 'I will grab them with my teeth and tear them to bits! I will throw trees on top of them and crush them!'

"Gluskabe drew Squirrel close to him and gently stroked his back until he was smaller than a rabbit. 'You are too angry and fierce to be a big animal,' he said. 'Now you can't hurt human beings. Go run away into the forest.'

"Gray Wolf walked over to Gluskabe and put his ear near Gluskabe's mouth.

"Again, Gluskabe whispered the Abenaki name for human beings. '*Alnobak!*'

"Wolf said, 'If they walk their way, I will walk mine. If they do not bother me, I will not bother them.'

"'That is good, Wolf,' said Gluskabe.

"Other animals approached Gluskabe and each gave the same answer when he whispered the name of human beings to them.

"Deer said, 'We will stay away from them. If they come to hunt us, we will run away.'

"Caribou said, 'We will stay away from them. If they come to hunt us, we will run away.'

"Elk said, 'We will stay away from them. If they come to hunt us, we will run away.'

"Gluskabe was satisfied that the animals and human beings could live together in the world, but then he spotted Dog. 'Dog! I almost forgot you! What will you do when the *Alnobak* arrive? Will you hunt them or harm them in any way?'

"Dog answered, 'I want to live with them. I want to curl up near their fires and share their food. I want to take care of their children and warn them if danger is near. I want to help them when they go hunting. I will risk my own life to save them. I will be their most loyal friend.'

"Gluskabe looked into Dog's eyes and saw that every word was true. He patted Dog on the head and said, 'My friend, you may have your wish. Go and live with the human people. Even though some may not deserve your friendship, you will be loyal to them and sleep near their fires.'

"And that is what happened, and that is how it is today." Eagle Wind leaned back and puffed again on his pipe. Peter Little Bear felt happy that he had Digger and Smells Bad. There were many dogs having their bellies rubbed that night.

Finally, as they did at the end of every day, the clan sang a song together, thanking the Great Spirit for making the world. Their songs spoke of the spirit inside all people, all animals, and every living thing. The Abenaki lived in harmony with nature, grateful for the plants they grew and gathered, for the animals they hunted for food, for the fresh, sparkling water they drank, and for the air they breathed.

4

A NEW FRIEND

As the days passed, the men and boys spent much of their time at the fishing weir and falls, catching salmon, shad, and other fish as they struggled their way upstream. Peter Little Bear liked to stand on a large flat rock near the opening in the weir and try to spear the fish as they swam by. He couldn't catch any the first few times he tried, but after some practice, he was able to spear two or three fish each day. He loved to catch fish, but he hated when he caught one of the slippery lamprey eels that also lived in the river. He thought they were ugly, with their long, slender bodies and big sucking mouths.

As the men caught the fish and tossed them onto the riverbank, the women, children, and elders used stone or iron knives to gut the fish, rinse them off, and lay them in the sun to dry. At the end of the day, when they returned to camp, the women cooked some of the fish right away for the evening meal. Most of the fish were hung from drying racks or smoked over a fire. The dried fish were good to eat in the winter, when hunting was difficult.

The men and boys also hunted for small animals in the woods surrounding the gardens. Swift Wolf taught Little Bear how to set clever traps to catch raccoons, woodchucks, and other animals that tried to eat the clan's maize, beans, and squash. Every part of the animal was used for some purpose. The women roasted some of the meat over the coals or boiled it with vegetables and **groundnuts** to make a stew. Much of the meat was cut into strips and smoked or dried for winter food. Bones were used to make tools. Sinew was used as tough cord. The women tanned the animal hides to make clothing and blankets.

Sometimes the men traded animal furs for the white settlers' iron tools—ax blades, hatchets, knives, and cooking pots. Although the clan was becoming very concerned by the number of colonists moving in along the lower river, life between the two groups remained peaceful. The Indians taught the newcomers how to hunt and fish, how to track animals, how to make snowshoes in the winter, and how to grow crops in the summer. Swift Wolf learned many English words and phrases, and he taught them to Morning Star, Little Bear, and others in the clan.

Because they knew life in the forest was changing, Swift Wolf and Morning Star had given Little

Bear an English name, Peter, to go with his Indian one. They hoped that having an English name would make it easier for their son to someday communicate with the strange, new people who were coming to their land. Peter Little Bear's parents were right.

One day, as he was fishing at the weir, Little Bear looked up and saw a boy standing on the bank above the falls, looking down at him. He was very surprised to see a colonist so young. The boy was about his size and had bright yellow hair, the color of cornsilk. He was barefoot but wore a shirt and homespun pants. During the summer, Little Bear wore only a **breechcloth**, a long piece of doeskin held up by a narrow belt around his waist.

The two boys stared at each other for a moment and then grinned, holding up their hands in a sign of peace. The blond boy scampered down to where Peter Little Bear was standing. He pointed to himself and said "Ebeneezer Wadleigh." The words were so strange to Little Bear's tongue that he couldn't pronounce them. The boy laughed, pointed to himself again, and said, "Eben." This time Little Bear got it

right. Then he tapped his own chest and said his full Indian name in the Abenaki language, "PeterAwasosis." Eben stumbled over the strange sounds like a tongue twister. Little Bear tapped his chest again and used his English name, Peter. Eben had no problem with that.

Little Bear signaled, "Let's swim" and Eben eagerly nodded yes in reply. They raced over to Little Bear's favorite swimming spot, Eben stripped off his clothes, and they both jumped into the water with a huge splash. Peter Little Bear was surprised to discover that Eben could barely swim, but he caught on quickly and they spent the afternoon laughing, splashing, and practicing their underwater handstands. At the end of the day, when they finally had to go their separate ways, neither of them wanted to leave. They waved goodbye to each other, and Eben hiked back toward the falls as Peter Little Bear walked the trail back to camp. He wondered if he would ever see the boy with cornsilk hair again.

That evening, Peter Little Bear told his parents about the boy he met at the falls. Swift Wolf nodded his head. "I know who that is. He has just come to live with Robert Wadleigh, the man who lives at the sawmill above the falls. I know Robert Wadleigh. He is a good man. He is honest and fair to our people. I will go with you tomorrow, Little Bear, and we will meet Robert Wadleigh and his boy together."

Over the next few days, Peter Little Bear learned that Robert Wadleigh had lived above the falls for many years. He had chosen the land near the falls to build his sawmill, a huge machine that used the power of the rushing Lamprey River to saw trees into thin boards. Other settlers bought the boards and used them to build their homes. Swift Wolf knew Robert Wadleigh very well—the two men were already friends. Peter Little Bear was nervous when he first met the heavyset white man, but the **miller** smiled broadly, extended his hand for Little Bear to shake, and said some friendly-sounding English words. Little Bear smiled shyly.

Little Bear learned that Eben was Robert Wadleigh's nephew. His father and mother had died during the family's rough ocean voyage from England to the town of **Portsmouth** in the New World. Since Eben was an orphan, he had no money to pay his way. He worked as a cabin boy for the rest of the trip and then made his way to his uncle's mill. His Uncle Robert gave him a home and made him his apprentice. That meant that Eben worked at the mill every day. He helped his uncle with whatever chores needed doing and learned as much as he could about the family business. Peter Little Bear thought it was natural for Eben to work at the mill, since he himself had to do daily chores around camp and work at the fishing weir.

Eben and Little Bear were very glad to have found each other. The boys in the clan were either too old or too young for Little Bear. He had grown bored playing games with Sleepy Eyes and Smoke Catcher.

Since Eben had just arrived at the sawmill, he didn't have any friends at all. He was the only child living at the mill, and he was lonely. Peter Little Bear and Eben met almost every day, either at the fishing weir or at the mill. As the days went by, Little Bear learned many English words and phrases, and he taught Eben some Abenaki words as well. Soon the boys were able to talk together.

Little Bear thought it was exciting to visit Eben at the sawmill, and Robert Wadleigh enjoyed having him around. The boys loved the smell of freshly cut lumber and liked to watch as the pile of sawdust mounded up under the saw. They were fascinated by the huge millwheel and how the rushing water that turned the wheel flowed through a wooden sluiceway. Little Bear and Eben would sit and watch the smaller pegged wheels turning together, creaking and groaning, geared to pull the giant saw blade up and down. Men pushed huge pine logs past the blade until finally a thin board broke loose. The mill worked day after day, turning hundreds of trees into boards for colonists' houses. Sometimes Peter Little Bear wondered if the white men planned to cut down the entire forest.

Eben's friendly manner and happy grin made him a welcome visitor at the Washucke camp. Little Bear taught Eben how to catch fish with his spear, and Swift Wolf was glad to see his son laughing with his new friend. One day, as the two boys were sitting in front of Little Bear's wigwam playing a pebble game, they noticed a crowd forming on the other side of camp. They ran over to investigate and there, standing in the center of the crowd with a smile on his face, was Little Bear's uncle, Joseph Running Deer. His trip to the White Mountains and back had lasted almost one moon, but he had found a stone for the new pestle. He handed the large piece of schist to Eagle Wind, who looked it over carefully.

"You chose well, Joseph Running Deer," he said. "This stone is just the right weight and shape. It will make a good pestle. I will start work on it today. Our new pestle will be ready soon."

Eagle Wind worked for many days, chipping, shaping, and rounding the stone until it was smooth and the tool was finished. The women used the pestle right away to grind acorns into meal. The acorns had been boiled many times to leach out the bitterness and then dried. The acorn meal was used to thicken a delicious fish stew. Before the feast, the clan gathered to sing songs and offer prayers, thanking the Mountain Spirit for giving them a new pestle. Then everyone sat together to eat and listen to Joseph Running Deer's stories of his long trip to the mountains. Even Smells Bad, the family's little dog, got extra scraps that night for making the long journey and returning home safely.

5

THE GARDEN

One of the most important jobs at the Washucke camp was growing maize and other vegetables in the clan's enormous garden. Over the many years, the clan had cleared a large, level growing field. The men had removed all the trees by burning them, chopping them down, and leaving the stumps to rot. Then they set fire to the remaining branches, brush, and weeds. When the fire finally burned itself out, the land was clear and the soil was loosened, enriched, and easier to prepare for planting.

When the weather was warm and the oak leaves had grown to the size of a squirrel's ear, the women knew it was time to plant crops. Since the garden was so large, everyone brought a hoe and helped work the soil. Their hoe blades were made from stone, large animal bones, carved wood, or heavy shells, and were lashed to long sticks. White Fawn was very proud this

year because she had her own little hoe—a short stick with a clamshell lashed to one end.

Once the ground was soft, the women scraped the soil into large mounds about two or three feet apart. They used pointed sticks to dig a hole in each mound and dropped one or two small fish into each hole. They usually used fish called **alewives** because they were so plentiful, but any small fish would do. Over the summer, the rotting fish fertilized the soil and helped the plants grow.

"Now we pile more soil over the fish," Morning Star explained to White Fawn. "Then we drop in three or four kernels of maize, cover it with more soil, and wait for it to grow. Once the maize has sprouted, we will come back and plant bean seeds in each hill. As the maize grows tall, the beanstalks will wind their way up and around the stalks of maize."

Between the mounds of maize and beans, the women planted pumpkin and squash seeds. The large leaves of those plants shaded the ground, kept it moist, and helped keep weeds from growing. All through the growing season, the women and girls pulled weeds, harvested crops, and prepared or stored the food. Boys and girls were also given the job of scaring big black crows and other birds out of the garden. Sleepy Eyes and Smoke Catcher liked to run between the rows of crops, banging sticks together and screaming as loud as they could. "Hey crows! Ayyyy! Fly away back to your nest!"

One day, as Little Bear and Eben were walking past the garden, Eben said, "Where I'm from, in England, men work in the gardens too."

"The men across the water do women's work?" Peter Little Bear laughed.

"It's honest work," Eben answered, "and you get to eat what you grow. I used to help my mother and father work in our garden at home. It was fun."

As the weeks passed, Eben spent more and more time at the Indian camp, fishing, swimming and playing with Peter Little Bear, and watching the Indian women planting and caring for the crops. He felt shy at first, but Morning Star's warm smile made him feel welcome. Sometimes he and Peter Little Bear would join White Fawn as she followed Morning Star through the forest. She taught them names of different plants, trees, nuts, and roots, and she explained how they were used for food or medicine.

Morning Star was the medicine woman or powwaw of the village. Usually it was a man who cured the ills of the clan, but Morning Star was very wise. She knew a great deal about making medicine and helping people when they were sick or injured. Sometimes she had visions or heard voices from the spirit world. Powwaws of the past would appear before her in dreams and offer guidance. Sometimes she could predict the future and warn the people of coming danger. She was very well-respected by their clan, and White Fawn hoped that someday she too could be a medicine woman.

Almost every day, the women and girls of the clan went into the forest to gather food. They knew where to find groundnuts, where to dig for tubers of the tall sunflower, and where to find the starchy roots of the yellow pond lily. They gathered wild artichokes and cooked them with meat for a tasty meal. In the summer, they picked strawberries, raspberries, blackberries, and blueberries and spread them in the sun to dry. Later the women would mix the dried berries with dried meat that had been ground up with the pestle. They would moisten the mix with fat from a deer or bear to make **pemmican**. This rich food could be carried on long journeys, and they would take it with them when they returned to their winter camps in the fall.

One hot afternoon as they headed back to camp, Morning Star stopped to cool off under a shade tree. She glanced up and said, "Oh! This is a **sassafras** tree. Do you see how its leaves have three different shapes?

Some leaves have one point, some have two rounded lobes, and some have three lobes." She chipped off a piece of root bark and held it up for the children to sniff. It smelled fragrant and sweet.

"I dry sassafras roots and use them to make a special tea," she explained. "The tea cures stomachaches, like the one Peter Little Bear had yesterday from eating too many chokecherries." She held her stomach and grimaced, and Eben knew just what she meant.

"We used sassafras as medicine in England, too," he said. "Sassafras bark sells for quite a bit of money. I mean, **wampum**!" When he used the Indian word for money, his friends nodded and understood.

They walked a bit farther until Morning Star stopped and chipped a bit of bark from a black cherry tree. "I boil this bark to make a medicine that soothes sore throats," she explained, holding her throat and pretending to cough. "It tastes very bad, and Peter Little Bear puts up a fight whenever he has to drink it, but it works every time." She pretended to taste the bark and made a sour face. The children laughed.

As the weeks went by, Eben learned more and more about using plants he could find in the wild. He learned to pick jewelweed and rub the juice from the stems on his mosquito bites or poison ivy rash to stop the itching. He watched the women and girls gather cattails and use every part of the plant in many different ways. They cooked the roots or dried them and used the new pestle to grind them into a sweet flour.

The young cattail shoots were good to eat raw or cooked. The women boiled the brown cattail heads in water, and they were delicious too. When the cattails were ripe, the women collected the golden pollen and mixed it with other flour for flavor or used it to thicken soups and stews. The cattail leaves were woven into mats that were used to cover the outside of their summer wigwams, or used inside to make a soft, clean floor. One day Morning Star surprised the children with toys fashioned from cattail leaves—a cattail doll for White Fawn and little cattail ducks for Peter Little Bear and Eben.

One afternoon, as a special treat, Morning Star gave each child a sparkling brown nugget and told them to let it melt in their mouths. The flavor was so sweet and good—Eben had never tasted anything like it. It was maple sugar candy, made the Indian way. In the very early spring, before leaving their winter camps in the Ossipee Mountains, the men cut diagonal gashes in sugar maple trees and fitted a hollowed-out elderberry twig or a carved wooden spout into the bottom of each gash. The sap ran out of the gashes, down the spouts, and was collected in birch bark containers. Then the sap was poured into a large clay pot or a tub made from a hollowed-out log. The men and women heated rocks in a fire and dropped the red-hot rocks into the sap to make it boil. It took a long, long time, but finally the sap boiled down to thick, sweet syrup. Boiled longer, it hardened into candy. Because it was so hard to make maple sugar candy, it was very precious. The children tried to make their nuggets last as long as possible, melting away on their tongues.

6

MOVING TO THE GREAT BAY

One day, after the clan had been at Washucke for more than two moons, Swift Wolf gathered the people around him and said, "The days are getting hot. The gardens have been planted. The maize and other crops look strong and healthy. It is a good time to go to the place the white men call the Great Bay. The older people will stay here in camp to take care of the small children and the gardens. The rest of us will go to the great water to hunt and fish."

This was one of Peter Little Bear's favorite adventures. As always, there would be plenty of work to do, but the work was fun and exciting. "Father," he asked, "can Eben come with us? Please? I've taught him how to fish, and you've seen how good he is with a spear."

Swift Wolf had never heard of such a thing. An English boy living the Indian way? He gathered the elders and asked them for advice. Some of the Indians distrusted the white men. They worried about the vast numbers of new people taking over their land. There were rumors of fighting between groups of colonists and other Indian tribes. But most of the Washucke clan felt comfortable with the newcomers and enjoyed trading with them and learning their ways. They decided that it was best for Swift Wolf to talk to Robert Wadleigh.

"It's good to see you, my friend," Robert Wadleigh said, as Swift Wolf and the boys approached the mill. The two men discussed the matter and Eben's uncle said, "Swift Wolf, I have seen you with your son and I see that you treat Eben like a son also. I feel the same way about Peter. I think it's a fine idea that Eben goes with you." The boys grinned at each other in excitement.

Early the next morning, the band started for the Bay. The trail was easy to follow. After fording the Lamprey River at a shallow place above the falls, they steadily made their way through the forest. Peter Little Bear and Eben walked together, carrying their spears and other supplies. They told tall tales about the fish they planned to catch.

"The fish I catch will be so big, we will have to build a new canoe just to carry it back to camp!" boasted Peter Little Bear.

"Well, the fish I catch will be so big, it will eat your fish!" laughed Eben.

The sun was high overhead when the Great Bay finally came into view. The tide was low, so the group stopped to gather mussels from the rocks that lined the shore. Then they moved out to a rocky peninsula that jutted out into the bay. It was a beautiful spot overlooking the water—a perfect place to camp. There was fresh water nearby, plenty of wildlife for hunting and fishing, and a cool breeze coming in off the bay that kept the mosquitoes away.

Instead of building sturdy wigwams, the women set up **tipis** for temporary shelters. Peter Little Bear, Eben, and a few of the younger boys wandered down to the water's edge. They hopped from one rock to the next, sliding on the slippery seaweed and falling in the water. It was a hot day, and soon they were up to their waists in the chilly salt water, laughing and splashing each other.

Morning Star called to them from above. "Little braves! The tide will be coming in soon, and the water will get deeper. Remember that the Great Bay is different from the river. All that slippery seaweed will be underwater soon."

The boys sloshed their way out of the water, laughing and throwing handfuls of seaweed at each other.

"Hey! Look at those!" Eben shouted. "What are they?"

Hundreds of horseshoe crabs lined the shore, moving back and forth like dark bowls turned upside down. Sleepy Eyes and Smoke Catcher ran along the beach, gathering the empty shells of dead crabs. They waved them at each other, pretending the sharp spiked tails were spearheads.

While the tide was still out, the women and girls carried woven baskets down to the water to look for shellfish. Some gathered oysters in the shallow water. Morning Star took White Fawn and some other girls out onto the **mudflats** and showed them how to use a stick and a big clamshell to dig for clams.

"Do you see this little hole in the sand?" she said, pointing. "A clam is down there!"

White Fawn was just about to start digging when a stream of sandy water shot out of the hole. She jumped back in surprise.

Morning Star and the other girls laughed. "That's just the clam spitting at you," her mother said. "Don't worry. It won't hurt you. See?" She pointed to other clam holes around them. "Lots of clams and lots of spitting!"

Everyone got busy digging for clams. White Fawn had just dropped her fourth clam into her basket when Peter Little Bear and Eben came by.

"Hey, Little Sister! We picked some flowers for you!" her brother said, grinning, and dumped an armful of slimy seaweed at her feet.

White Fawn smiled to herself and said, "Well, I have something special to show you too! See here? This hole in the sand? Look close and you can see the ocean!"

Peter Little Bear knelt down and peered into the hole. "I don't see any...hey!" A spray of water hit him right in the eye.

Eben, White Fawn, and the other girls doubled over with laughter.

"Oh! Oh!" Eben's face was bright red from laughing. "Are you sure your name is Peter Little Bear?" he gasped. "I think we should call you Peter Spit in the Eye from now on!" He fell down, laughing and rolling around in the sand.

Peter Little Bear stood up laughing and wiping his face. Then he grabbed a handful of seaweed, dumped it on Eben's head, and said, "I think we should call you Eben Slimy Hair!" Both boys took off, racing toward the water to rinse off.

Later everyone feasted on steamed clams, mussels, and oysters. The women shucked the rest of the catch and strung the shellfish on long, thin reeds that they hung over the fire. The smoked fish would keep for many moons and be good food during the winter.

"Little Bear and Eben!" called Morning Star. "Make yourselves useful and carry these baskets of empty shells over to the shell pile."

Eben was surprised to see how large the mound of old shells and bones along the shoreline was. The Indian clan had come to this place for hundreds of seasons, gathering shellfish, hunting for seals, and fishing.

The next morning, a thin mist hung over the water and the air was cool. After breakfast, Swift Wolf and some of the other men set out to retrieve their dugout canoes. Last fall, the men had filled the canoes with heavy stones and had sunk them in a hidden spot to keep them safe. When they dragged the canoes out of the water to dry, Eben was amazed by their size. Each canoe had been carved from the trunk of a very large tree. The men had used axes to carve and shape the bottom and sides of each canoe. To hollow out the inside, they built many small fires on the top side of the tree. When the wood was black and charred, they used stone scrapers or heavy clamshells to scrape out the burned part. Then they built more fires and repeated the whole process. It took almost one moon, thirty days, to make one dugout canoe, and it was a team effort.

"Why don't you use birch bark canoes?" asked Eben. "I've seen some of your braves making them, and they seem so much easier to make."

"They are," nodded Swift Wolf, "but they're too lightweight to use out on the big water, and they only hold a few braves. Our dugout canoes carry many people at once, and they handle well in the tall waves."

As the days passed, everyone stayed busy with chores of some kind. The women and girls walked through the salt marshes, gathering marsh grass. The grass was long and tough and had a wonderful sweet smell. Back at camp, Morning Star taught White Fern how to split the grass blades into long, fine strips. They left the strips out to dry and then packed them into tight bundles to take home.

"This winter, I will teach you to weave a beautiful basket with this grass," Morning Star promised her daughter. "How would you like to decorate it?"

White Fawn thought for a while. "I want to use two different colors of grass to make a pattern. And I want to decorate it with colored porcupine quills and seashells. And maybe some feathers!"

"And when the weather gets warm again," said Morning Star, smiling, "you can use the basket to gather strawberries."

Out on the water, the men worked hard, fishing and hunting. They would float their canoes in the shallow water and use sharp harpoons on long thin shafts to spear lobsters. They hunted the seals that sunned themselves on rocks close to shore. In the deeper water, the men fished for striped bass, sturgeon, and cod. When Eben saw the huge fish they brought back to camp, he understood why the men used the heavy dugout canoes.

"Peter, these fish are as big as we are!" he said.

Little Bear nodded his head. "Remember when you said your fish was going to eat my fish? You were right! These fish really *do* eat other fish!"

7

A TRIP TO PORTSMOUTH

Early one morning, Swift Wolf told Peter Little Bear and Eben, "Joseph Running Deer and I are taking some beaver **pelts** to trade with the white men. How would you like to come along and see the giant boats with their huge white sails?"

Peter Little Bear had never been to the harbor before, and Eben hadn't been there since he arrived in the New World a few months ago, so they were both very excited. They rushed through their morning chores and soon joined Swift Wolf, Joseph Running Deer, and some of the other men and older boys in the dugout canoe. The tide had just turned and was going out. The men were able to use the swift current to leave the Great Bay and eventually paddle their canoe down the **Piscataqua River** until they reached the harbor. They secured the canoe along the shoreline, hefted their loads of pelts, and headed toward the place the white men called Portsmouth.

Soon the colonists' wooden houses came into view, and the path turned into a narrow, rock-studded road. As they walked, Peter Little Bear's eyes grew wide with wonder. Wherever he looked, he saw an amazing new sight. He had never seen so many big houses and pale-faced colonists before. Everyone seemed busy and in a hurry.

Eben had seen similar sights in England. "The houses in England are much finer than these," he said. "But my family had very little money and we owned no land. I think my life here will be better."

A huge animal plodded by, pulling a two-wheeled wagon loaded down with supplies.

"Father!" Peter Little Bear exclaimed, jumping out of the way. "What is *that*?"

"The white men call that an ox," his father answered. "It is very strong and can pull very heavy loads."

"And it would hurt a lot if it stepped on your toe!" chuckled Eben.

The closer they walked to the great ships, the noisier and busier the town became. Peter Little Bear felt a little frightened, but when he looked up at Swift Wolf, he relaxed. He could tell that his father felt at ease and confident. Peter Little Bear was proud of his father, his uncle, and the other braves as they walked through the town, but it was hard to tell what the colonists were thinking as the Indians walked by. Some seemed curious. Some looked worried and afraid, having heard about Indian attacks on some of the inland settlements. Some people gaped at Eben, an English boy walking with a band of Indians. But most people simply ignored them and went about their business.

Finally the group came to where the big ships were docked in the harbor. The great white sails of one ship snapped and billowed in the wind as it moved up the Piscataqua River. Swift Wolf pointed to the enormous pine logs that floated along the shore.

"Do you boys see the three white gashes cut into each of those tree trunks?" he asked. "The white men use their axes to cut that mark into the very tallest

pine trees. They call it the **King's Broad Arrow**, and say that once marked, those trees belong to their great sachem across the water."

This made no sense to Peter Little Bear or anyone else in the Washucke clan. The Indians believed that the land was shared by every living thing—people, animals, insects, and plants—and that no one could own any of it.

Swift Wolf pointed to the huge ships anchored in the harbor. "See there? The tall trees piled on the big boats with white sails? Robert Wadleigh told me that those trees will be taken across the water and will be used as **masts** to hold the sails of other boats."

It made Peter Little Bear sad to think of the mighty trees being cut down and sent so far away. His forest was changing, and he didn't like it very much.

Swift Wolf and Joseph Running Deer talked with a white man about trading the beaver pelts they had brought. The man talked loudly and made wide gestures with his arms and hands. Little Bear's father and uncle stood quietly, waiting for a deal to be decided. Finally they smiled. The trading party handed over the piles of pelts. In exchange, they received four metal knives, a metal hatchet, a large cooking kettle, a bundle of wool cloth, and many strings of purple and white shell beads, called **wampum**. The Indians used wampum to make jewelry and to decorate their clothing, and both Indians and colonists used the beads as a form of money.

Half the day had passed and the tide had turned. It was time for the group to return to their canoe and ride the current upriver and across the Bay to get back to their fishing campsite. Morning Star and the other women were very happy to see the new knives, kettle, and cloth. Swift Wolf gave White Fawn a present—a necklace with two pieces of wampum on it, one purple and one white.

That night, everyone feasted on a rich fish and vegetable stew. Later, at the campfire, the trading party took turns telling stories about their trip to Portsmouth and what they liked best. Swift Wolf spoke about how they traded the beaver pelts for goods and wampum. Joseph Running Deer told the clan about the huge boats with their billowing sails. By the time it was the boys' turn to tell their stories, they had already fallen fast asleep.

The clan stayed at their seaside camp for many days, gathering shellfish, hunting, and fishing. Peter Little Bear and Eben noticed that they weren't the only ones looking for fish. Stately blue herons waded in the shallow water along the shore. They were so quiet and patient, barely moving until a fish swam nearby and then—flash!—their long necks and sharp bills would spear an unsuspecting fish. When the boys ventured too near, the giant birds would jump into the air, gracefully spreading their huge wings, and fly away.

High in the towering pine trees, majestic bald eagles built gigantic nests and watched for fish in the waters below. The boys loved to watch the eagles swoop down and snatch fish right out of the water with their enormous claws. Then they would swoop away again, flapping their powerful wings as they carried off their heavy load.

Little Bear's favorite birds were ospreys. Smaller than eagles, ospreys built nests in the very tops of trees. They hovered and soared high in the sky, scanning the water for fish. When an osprey spotted a fish, it would dive straight toward it, headfirst, righting itself at the very last second to seize the fish with its sharp **talons**. Sometimes an eagle would chase the osprey into the air to make it drop its fish. Then the eagle would swoop around and catch the fish as it fell from the sky.

There was so much to see and do that the weeks seemed to fly by, and another moon had passed. It was time for the clan to pack up their supplies and return to the gardens and village at Washucke. The air was growing cool, and the leaves in the forest had started to turn orange, red, and yellow. Flocks of birds could be seen overhead, flying south for the winter. Bushy-tailed squirrels ran through the forest carrying fat acorns in their mouths, stashing their food away for winter. Eben and Peter Little Bear were sad to say goodbye to the fishing camp and the Great Bay. Camping together had made them even closer—the very best of friends.

8

MEETING THE GREAT SACHEM

One morning in early autumn, Peter Little Bear woke to find Swift Wolf and Morning Star already up and dressed in their finest clothes.

"Peter Little Bear!" Morning Star said, smiling, "Get up quickly and have something to eat! We are taking you on a trip today."

Peter Little Bear rubbed his eyes and stretched. "A trip? Where are we going?" White Fawn was still asleep, curled up under a warm deer hide, hugging her little cornhusk doll. "Is White Fawn coming too?"

"No, White Fawn will stay with Grandfather," Morning Star answered. "Today, we are going to meet the great sachem, **Moharimet**. His **lodge** is on top of a high hill, near the place the white men call Dover. It is a long walk—too long for your sister's short legs. We will spend the night there and return to Washucke tomorrow."

"It is a great honor to meet with such a wise sachem," added Swift Wolf. "We have important things to discuss with him. Now that you are growing up, we thought it was time for you to learn more about the world."

Peter Little Bear was very excited as he washed up and rushed through his breakfast. When the trio was ready, they headed north on the Pentucket Trail. Eventually the path split, and they took a second trail that went by the **Pond of Turtles**. The sun was low in the sky when they finally reached Moharimet's camp. The great sachem was seated next to a small campfire, smoking his pipe and talking with some other adults. He wore a beautiful necklace of bear claws and porcupine quills, and had a deerskin cloak around his shoulders. He raised his hand in greeting as Swift Wolf and Morning Star approached him. Peter Little Bear felt nervous about meeting Moharimet but was proud of his strong and wise parents, who spoke for his clan.

They took a seat by the fire and the group discussed the growing troubles between the colonists and the Indian tribes. More and more white men arrived every day, moving into the coastal land and pushing inland in all directions. The Indians could see they were losing their hunting and fishing grounds and this worried them. They believed that the Great Spirit created the land for all people and all animals to live together in peace. They believed that the land belonged to everyone.

The white colonists had a very different view. They came from countries where land was divided up and sold to those who could afford it. Many of the colonists hadn't owned any land at all, and came to the New World hoping for a better life. When they arrived, they simply claimed empty land or bought it cheaply from the Indians. The Indians sold or traded their land to the colonists without understanding what that really meant. They were asked to sign complicated contracts or treaties written in a language they didn't speak and couldn't read. Sometimes they signed with an X and sometimes the colonists signed for them, guessing at the spelling of their names.

Moharimet said, "There are greater troubles coming. The war that the white men called **King Philip's War** is over. It has been almost five years since **Metacom**, the powerful sachem of the **Wampanoag** tribe, was killed and the war ended. But there are still many bands of fierce warriors who are very angry at the white men for taking over so much Indian land. They are angry at Indians who live peacefully with the white men. These warriors come mostly from the north now, setting fire to houses and settlements. They kill many people—English, Abenaki, men, women, and children. Those they don't kill, they take captive."

Peter Little Bear moved a little closer to Morning Star.

Swift Wolf said, "The land at Washucke is owned by Robert Wadleigh. He told me that the town of

Dover gave him the land all around his mill, that it belongs to him now. But he said we are welcome to stay—to hunt, to fish, and to live at Washucke as our ancestors did. Our lives, so far, are peaceful."

Moharimet nodded and stared into the fire. "Today it is peaceful. But many of our people are leaving our land near the Great Water. Many are moving farther north and west, where the white men are fewer and we are safe from warring tribes."

The great sachem talked longer with Swift Wolf and Morning Star, but Peter Little Bear didn't hear them. He was thinking about how much he loved Washucke and their fishing camp on the Great Bay. He let his mind wander to fishing at the falls, hunting in the woods, and spending time with Eben. He was startled when his father tapped his chest, saying, "This is my son, Peter Little Bear. He may be sachem of our clan some day."

Moharimet nodded slowly at Little Bear, sizing him up. "Your job will be a hard one, young brave," he said quietly. "The troubles you will face I cannot imagine. Your world will be different from mine. Learn well the lessons your parents teach you, and you will grow to be a strong and wise leader."

9

THE CAVE IN THE WOODS

A few days after they had visited the great sachem, Moharimet, Swift Wolf said, "Peter Little Bear, there are some places I want to show you. Bring your fishing line and come along with me."

"Can Eben come?" Little Bear asked.

"Not this time," his father answered.

They headed north on the Pentucket Trail as it wound first along the shore of the Lamprey River and then across a small stream. Peter Little Bear asked his father if they were going to fish on the river, but Swift Wolf said, "No. I want to show you a pond I know of. It has plenty of big white perch that are very good to eat."

They left the trail and followed a smaller path. After a while, Swift Wolf said, "We are almost at the pond, but first, I want to show you a special place—a place you should know about." Little Bear eagerly followed his father through the underbrush. Soon they came to a small, rocky cliff. It was surrounded by trees and ferns, and the rock wall was covered with crunchy flakes of green **lichen**.

His father said, "This is the place. Climb up the rock face and see what you find."

Little Bear was a good climber and had no trouble scrambling toward the top of the cliff. Just below the top, he found a small cave. He crawled inside, turned around, and called down, "Father! This cave is a perfect hiding place!"

Swift Wolf smiled. "I know. It is just big enough and deep enough for one person. My father showed me this cave when I was a boy. I was waiting for the right time to show you."

Peter Little Bear poked his head out of the cave, and said, "Why is now the right time?"

"Your mother had a powerful dream last night," his father answered. "Her dream was filled with visions and sounds of fighting, and feelings of fear and anger. Faces came to her in the dream—some faces she knew and some she didn't know. She saw your face, and she saw fear in your eyes. She also saw a small cave, but couldn't see what was in it or where it was. When she told me her dream, I knew I must show you this place."

Little Bear shivered in the warm air, thinking of his mother's dream. What could it mean? Why was there fear in his eyes? As he carefully made his way down the rock face, Swift Wolf said, "Take a moment to look around. I want to be sure you remember how to find this cave again."

Little Bear did as he was told. His eyes scanned the trees, the shape of the land, and the vegetation. He walked around the little cliff to see how it looked from the top and from the sides. He remembered how different the forest had looked when he and Swift Wolf had tried to find the lost pestle. He didn't want to be confused again looking for a spot in the woods.

Father and son continued through the forest,

down a hill, and in a short time they came to the pond. It was a beautiful place, with tall pine trees growing by the shore. They found a good spot in a small clearing and threw in their fishing lines. Before long, Peter Little Bear felt a tug on his line.

"Hey!" He jumped up and started pulling in his line. "I've got one!"

The fish were biting, and they soon had a nice catch of fish. Swift Wolf said, "These perch swam all the way upstream from the Great Bay, where White Fawn found all those clams."

Peter Little Bear chuckled, remembering "Spit in the Eye."

The afternoon sun warmed their skin and made them feel lazy. Swift Wolf stretched, yawned, and pulled in his fishing line. "We've got enough fish for today," he said. "Let's go for a swim."

He stood up and dove into the water, swimming powerfully across the pond toward a small island. Watching his father's smooth strokes, Peter Little Bear called out, "Maybe your name should be Swift Otter!" He laughed and dove in after him, swimming hard.

Swift Wolf smiled at his son. "And look at Little Bear, swimming strong through the water!" They sat together at the edge of the island, letting the sun dry their skin. After a while, Peter Little Bear jumped up and tried skipping small rocks across the surface of the pond. One...two... three hops before disappearing into the water. Swift Wolf gave it a try.

One...two... three...four-five-six hops! Peter Little Bear hoped that some day his arms would be as strong as his father's.

"You and Eben have had a good summer together, haven't you?" Swift Wolf asked.

The boy nodded. "Yes." He threw another rock. Two skips.

"I have become good friends with his uncle, as well," continued Swift Wolf. "He is a fair and honest man. We trust and respect each other. His ways are very different from mine, but in our hearts, we are very much the same."

"That's how I feel about Eben," Peter Little Bear answered. "I know he came from across the water. I know he lives in a big house and eats strange food and speaks a strange language. But when we're together, I feel like he is my brother."

Swift Wolf put his strong hand on the boy's shoulder. "That is what counts, my son," he said. "Our world is changing so fast, in ways we don't always understand. The feelings in your heart are what really matter."

As the sun dipped toward the horizon, the pair swam back to shore, gathered up their catch, and started back through the woods. Their feet moved quickly and silently over the soft forest floor. As they passed the cliff and cave, Peter Little Bear scanned the area once more, memorizing how the forest looked from this new direction in the late afternoon light.

They rejoined the main path and in a short while, arrived in camp. That night, there was a feast of perch cooked with beans from the garden and wild artichokes that White Fawn had gathered with her mother. Later, as a very tired Peter Little Bear drifted off to sleep, he smiled to himself. It had been a wonderful day spent with his father.

Weeks passed and the cool air of early autumn gave way to cold winds and leafless trees. Autumn was the clan's most important hunting season, and the men spent many days tracking deer, bear, moose, and other animals. Harvest time had come and gone, and the clan felt well-prepared for the long winter ahead. The women burned the dried leaves and stalks left in the garden, rolled up the cattail mats that covered the wigwams, and the families started the long hike back to their winter camps.

Before Swift Wolf's family left, they stopped at the mill to say goodbye to Robert Wadleigh and Eben.

"You're coming back, aren't you?" Eben asked.

Peter Little Bear looked up at Morning Star. She smiled at him and nodded yes. Then the family shouldered their gear and headed back up the Pentucket Trail.

10

THE BATTLE AT WHEELWRIGHT'S POND

The clan returned to the Washucke camp on the Lamprey River year after year. Each spring, Eben and Peter Little Bear surprised each other with how much they'd grown. By 1690, both boys were almost men. Eben was short, stocky, and very muscular from the work in his uncle's mill. Beneath his tangle of blond, curly hair, his freckled face was quick to break into a smile. Peter Little Bear, meanwhile, had grown tall and slim like his father, with powerful muscles and black, shiny hair. The boys had known each other for eight years, and they truly felt like brothers. They spent hours each day talking, working, and playing together.

White Fawn surprised Eben too, by growing into a slender young woman with dark, intelligent eyes and long, black hair that she usually wore in braids. She had been a good student. She knew where to find even the rarest plants and how to turn them into medicines to cure the injured or the sick. Eben still had a strong interest in natural medicine as well. He and White Fawn often went on walks together, gathering roots and bark samples, as White Fawn explained how they were used. Somehow, Eben always managed to make her laugh.

Life on the Lamprey River was not nearly as peaceful as it had been in the past. Settlers continued to stream into the area, taking over vast tracts of land, building houses, and using the river for their own purposes. This deeply angered some of the Indian tribes. Bands of warriors from enemy tribes roamed the seacoast area, and the colonists were very nervous. Members of Peter Little Bear's clan were nervous too, since the warriors killed Abenaki as well as settlers. Robert Wadleigh spoke often with Swift Wolf and Morning Star, sharing rumors and news.

One hot July day, the two boys decided to do some fishing. It had been a dry summer, the river was too low to run the mill, and Eben was able to leave. As the boys set off up the trail, Peter Little Bear said, "I know where there's a nice pond where we can catch some perch and then go swimming. My father took me there once, but I haven't been back in many years."

They left the main trail and headed toward the pond. They stayed alert and listened carefully as they traveled farther from the mill. There had been a series of Indian raids on the colonists in this area, and some people had been killed. This worried the boys enough to put them on their guard but, being young, they eventually relaxed and forgot their worries.

About a mile from the pond, Little Bear remembered the cave. "Eben! I've got something to show you!" He looked around and then veered off into the woods, heading for the cliff. As they approached the lichen-covered rock wall, Little Bear said, "Go on! Climb up there and see what you find."

Eben clambered up and exclaimed, "Peter! It's an oven!"

The Indian boy laughed. "An oven? What's that?"

"It's what we call a small cave in England," Eben replied, crawling into the cave and looking down. "Let's call this Peter's Oven. We can use it as our secret hideaway for buried treasure!" Eben's Uncle Robert had told him about pirates, and Eben was convinced that if he dug enough holes, he would someday find gold doubloons.

The boys hiked on until they reached the pond. Eben was about to venture into a clearing when Peter Little Bear grabbed him by the shirt and pulled him down.

"Shhh!" he whispered. "Don't make a sound!"

The boys crouched behind some bushes near the shore.

"What is it?" Eben whispered. "What did you hear?"

"I heard voices coming from across the pond," his friend whispered back. "Listen!"

Then Eben heard them too. He poked his head above the bushes and then ducked down quickly. "Warriors!" he whispered. "On the other side!"

Peter Little Bear looked at his friend and shook his head in wonder. "You have bright yellow hair. Are you poking your head up to give them target practice?"

He carefully parted the bushes in front of him and peeked through. Sure enough, a large band of warriors was gathered on the far side of the pond. Some were fishing, while others were resting or standing guard nearby.

"Who are they?" Eben whispered.

"I don't know," Little Bear whispered back. "They are from a tribe I don't recognize. Their faces are painted for war!"

Eben carefully peeked through the bushes and agreed that the warriors looked very fierce and dangerous.

Suddenly gunshots rang out and two of the Indians fell to the ground. The others grabbed their rifles and ran in all directions, disappearing behind trees and brush. Another loud shot was followed by a splash as a white man collapsed into the water along the shoreline. Then it seemed as if colonists and Indians were everywhere. Eben guessed there were at least one hundred colonists, but it was hard for him to tell

how many Indian warriors. The boys could hear screams of pain from every direction as bullets found their marks. The battle raged all around them. The air filled with the pungent smell of gunpowder, and the acrid smoke stung the boys' eyes. The fighting raged on with both sides dodging from tree to tree in close combat.

Eben's face was white with fear. "Peter!" he hissed, "We could be shot by either side. You're Indian, I'm English. They won't care who we are—they'll just shoot us!"

"You're right," his friend hissed back. "Let's get out of here!"

Staying as close to the ground as possible, the boys crawled through the dense underbrush. Slowly, they made their way up the bank and farther up the hill until they left the fighting behind. They could still hear the shouts of the settlers and the war cries of the Indians, but they felt they were mostly out of danger and breathed a little easier. They stood up, quietly made their way to the path, and then started running as fast as they could. The sounds of the battle grew faint, and all was well until Peter Little Bear glanced behind him. His right foot caught on a root and he came crashing to the ground, badly twisting his ankle.

"Aghh! Eben! Wait!"

Eben turned to see his friend lying on the ground, writhing in pain. He rushed back and helped him up, but the twisted ankle would support no weight. Eben got Little Bear's arm around his shoulders and half dragged, half carried him up the slope. At the top, both boys collapsed on the ground, gasping from heat and exhaustion.

"We've got to do something about your leg," said Eben. "The swelling is getting worse. Can you move it at all?"

Peter Little Bear tried, but a deep, sharp pain stopped him immediately. "No," he answered, miserably. "I think it might be broken."

Eben took off his shirt and handed it to his friend.

"Rip this into long strips that we can use for bandages." He glanced around them. "Ah! Here we go." Using his pocketknife, he cut two curved pieces of birch bark from a nearby tree, each about the size of his hand. "Your ankle is already pretty swollen," he said, "and I know this will hurt some, but I'm going to try to bandage it so it won't move as much. Morning Star told me that's the best thing to do for a twisted leg or arm."

He placed the pieces of bark on either side of Little Bear's swollen ankle. Then he wrapped strips from his shirt around the bark and around Little Bear's foot and leg to hold it in place. When he was done, Peter Little Bear couldn't move his injured foot at all.

His tired face creased into a smile. "That feels a lot better, Eben. I'm glad you listened so well to my mother's lessons. You might become a powwaw yourself someday."

Eben grinned briefly, but then his face clouded with worry. "Peter, I don't think I can carry you all the way home. Can you wait here while I go get help?"

"I think the fighting is getting closer," Peter Little Bear said. "We should keep going." He grabbed a nearby tree and hauled himself to a standing position. "Aghh!" he gasped, almost collapsing from pain. "Eben, I can't make it home! Can you help me get to the cave? I could hide in there."

Keeping Little Bear's weight off his hurt foot, the two boys hobbled through the forest to the top of the little cliff. Eben helped his friend get as close to the cave entrance as possible, and with his last bit of strength, Little Bear struggled his way inside. The cave was full of dry leaves, which served as a soft bed. He squirmed as far back as he could until Eben couldn't see him at all. Then Eben glanced around to make sure the coast was clear and started running down the trail toward home.

11

THE RESCUE

Sweat poured down Eben's face and stung his eyes as he raced along the Pentucket Trail. He was a strong runner, and his fear helped him cover the distance to his uncle's mill very quickly.

"Uncle Robert! Uncle Robert!" he gasped. "There's a battle at a big pond north of here! Lots of people are getting shot, and Peter fell and hurt his foot. He's hiding in an oven and needs help!"

Mr. Wadleigh and Eben rushed to the Indian village and found Swift Wolf and Morning Star. Again. Eben told his story about Little Bear's fall and the ongoing battle.

"Peter's hiding in an oven…I mean, a little cave," Eben repeated. "He can't walk at all, and the fighting was getting closer!"

The two men knew at once that the pond was the one the white men called **Wheelwright's Pond**. They remained calm, trying to decide what to do. Swift Wolf said, "If the white men see me, they will surely shoot me, and if the warriors see you, they will shoot us both."

"That's true," said Robert Wadleigh, "but we've got no choice. Eben, go back to the mill and spread the word that there's a battle at Wheelwright's Pond. Swift Wolf and I will go fetch Peter."

A look of deep trust passed between the two men as they started out, moving swiftly up the trail. They stopped from time to time, listening for sounds of battle. As they approached the cave, they could hear gunshots nearby. They crept up to the base of the cliff and Swift Wolf gave a low whistle like the sound of a bird. An answering whistle came right back, so they knew Peter Little Bear was there.

Without a sound, Robert Wadleigh made his way around to the top of the cliff as Swift Wolf climbed to the mouth of the cave. Seeing his father's face, Peter Little Bear wanted to shout with joy, but Swift Wolf signaled for silence. As gently as he could, he helped slide his son out of the cave and handed him up to Robert Wadleigh's waiting arms. Then Robert lifted the boy onto Swift Wolf's back, and they started down the trail toward the falls. The sounds of battle once again faded in the distance, but the men kept up their hurried pace. After a few miles, Robert Wadleigh noticed Swift Wolf was slowing down.

"Swift Wolf," he said, "let me carry Peter for a

while." Swift Wolf gratefully loaded his son onto the miller's strong back, and the band of three set off again. It was late afternoon when they finally reached home. Morning Star was waiting anxiously, but she smiled with relief and pride when she saw the bandage Eben had made.

"Your friend learned his lessons well," she said, as she gently cut away the bandage and examined Little Bear's ankle. "The bone is broken, so keeping your foot from moving was the best thing to do. It will take some time, Little Bear, but your ankle will be strong again."

A few days later, details of the battle finally came to the families at the Wadleigh Mill. A band of **Kennebec** Indians had been attacking settlements around the seacoast. They burned many homes, and either killed people or took them captive. They spared no one, slaughtering Indians as well as colonists.

Word went out that the band was camping on the shores of Wheelwright's Pond. Two companies of men from **Oyster River**, led by Captain Floyd and Captain Wiswall, set out to find them. The men hiked down the Pentucket Trail and crept up to the edge of Wheelwright's Pond. There, they found the Indians fishing. The colonists spread out around the shoreline and opened fire.

The battle raged for several hours with close-range gunfire and hand-to-hand fighting. Both warriors and colonists ducked behind big trees to reload their guns and stealthily peer around the trunks, searching for the enemy. The day was desperately hot and the colonists, dressed in heavy homespun clothes, suffered terribly from the heat. Several men died of heat exhaustion.

Finally, both sides gave up the fight. The Indians withdrew, taking their dead with them. The colonists came back to help the wounded and bury their dead. Many on both sides were killed or wounded. Captain Wiswall and fifteen of his men died in the battle. The date was July 6, 1690.

The boys enjoyed their time together as the rest of the summer passed. Peter Little Bear's ankle healed fairly quickly, and he was able to hobble around, first with the help of a long stick, and eventually on his own. When autumn came and it was time for the Washucke clan to move to their winter campgrounds, he was able to carry a heavy load of supplies. His ankle was strong and his leg did not hurt him, though he walked with a slight limp for many years to come.

The two families said goodbye once again and wished each other well through the long, cold winter season. Eben hiked alongside his friend for a short way. Then the boys parted company along the Pentucket Trail, one heading back to the mill and the other heading toward the mountains.

12

ONE LAST VISIT HOME, 1700

Peter Little Bear's clan never returned to the Washucke camp. Each spring, Eben waited for his friend to appear, but he never did. Each growing season, as the snow melted and the weather warmed, Peter Little Bear hoped his clan would return to their springtime camp along the Lamprey River, but that never came to pass. Settlers from Europe continued to pour into the coastal area and move inland, changing life forever for the Indian tribes. The colonists built houses, mills, and other structures along the shoreline and on the riverbanks. This eventually affected the wildlife in the rivers and forest. Debris from the mills contaminated the water, and fish weren't nearly as plentiful. Animals became scarce from overhunting.

The settlers were eager to trade their kettles, knives, axes, and cloth for animal pelts. Year after year, the Indian men spent more time trapping beaver and other small animals for trade and less time fishing and hunting for large game. The women spent more time cleaning and tanning animal hides and less time growing crops and gathering wild plants. As gardens were neglected and food supplies shrank, the clans and tribes had less to eat, and surviving the winters was hard.

The Indians' traditional lands were disappearing. Clans returned to their warm-weather camps only to find them taken over by a new community of white settlers. Angry tribes of Indians continued to attack white settlements as well as Indian camps. The colonists reacted with violence, and relations between Indians and settlers went from dangerous to deadly. Peter Little Bear's clan was forced to move far away from Washucke to find good hunting and fishing grounds in a place where they could live in peace. Whether they moved west to the Adirondacks or north into Canada, no one at the Wadleigh Mill knew for sure.

Many years after the Battle at Wheelwright's Pond, a tall Indian brave appeared at the Wadleigh Mill. He wore fine deerskin leggings and a headband decorated with beads and eagle feathers. Around his neck was a necklace of bear claws and porcupine quills. His walk was strong and confident with just a hint of a limp.

Wadleigh Falls was now a bustling community built around the sawmill. Nothing looked familiar to him, and no one knew who he was. He saw white men

but no Indians. He approached the mill and asked an old, white-haired man standing outside, "Do you know a man named Eben Wadleigh? Do you know where I can find him?"

The man squinted up at the Indian and studied his face. "Peter? Peter, can it be you? It's me, Robert Wadleigh!"

The men exchanged a warm embrace.

"It is good to see you after all these years," said Little Bear. "And Eben?" He looked around him. "Where can I find him?"

Robert Wadleigh shook his head. "I'm sorry, Peter, but Eben is gone. When he turned twenty-one, his apprenticeship at the mill ended. He decided to become a doctor and needed more schooling. With our blessing, he married and moved south to the city of Boston. I'm sorry you missed him, Peter. I know he wanted to see you. He waited and hoped for your return, year after year."

Peter Little Bear nodded sadly and turned to go.

"Peter!" Mr. Wadleigh stopped him. "How is your family? And the rest of the Washucke clan?"

"Our clan is smaller in number, and each year we must travel farther north to find good hunting and fishing and to live in peace. My parents are well, and White Fawn is married and has a child. She continues to learn from my mother, and hopes one day to become a powwaw. I learn from both my father and my mother. My parents tell me that I will be sachem one day."

Robert Wadleigh nodded his head. "And you, Peter?" he asked. "Do you have a family of your own?"

Peter Little Bear smiled. "I have a wife and a son. My wife's name is Laughing Water. My son's name is Eben Running Bear."

He lifted his eyes and scanned the changed landscape and busy town one last time. "I wish you well, Robert Wadleigh," he said.

"I wish you well, Peter Little Bear," the older man replied.

Then the tall Indian brave turned and walked away from the mill and back into the forest. He headed down the Pentucket Trail and never returned to Washucke again.

LEE, NEW HAMPSHIRE, 1969

As more settlers from Europe moved to the sea-coast area, life changed for the Woodland Indians. Abenaki tribes were forced to move farther and farther north into Maine and Canada. By the end of the seventeenth century, the Washucke camp at Wadleigh Falls had been abandoned. The falls, however, had become a very busy place. Over the years, more mills were built and run at Wadleigh Falls: a sawmill, a grist mill (to grind corn or other grains), a drug mill, a cider mill, and a shoe factory. Each year, more people arrived, built houses, and started businesses. What started out as an Indian camp and a small colonial settlement grew into Lee, New Hampshire—a home for thousands of people.

About 300 years after the Washucke clan camped at the falls, on a sunny day in 1969, Lloyd Stevens, the road agent for the Town of Lee, was grading the dirt road on the New Town Plains in northern Lee. Suddenly, he heard a loud "clang!" He stopped the grader and got down to see what he'd hit. The grader blade had turned up a large, strange-looking stone. Mr. Stevens picked it up and cleaned it off.

The lost pestle was found.

ANNOTATED GLOSSARY

Abenaki—"land where the sun first bathes the earth in light;" "dawn land." The Abenaki Indians were called the People of the Dawn because they were first to see the rising sun each day. The Abenaki lived in parts of New Hampshire, Maine, Vermont, and Canada. The Abenaki Confederation includes the following tribes: Amaseconti, Androscoggin, Kennebec, Maliseet, Ouarastegouiak, Passamaquoddy, Patsuiket, Penobscot, Pigwacket, Rocameca, Sokoni, Wewenoc, Micmac, and Pennacook.

alewife—a small, silvery fish in the herring family that spawns.

Alnobak—Abenaki word for "human people." (Also spelled Alnbôk or Aln8bak. The ô and 8 are symbols for a "nasal o" pronunciation.)

breechcloth (sometimes spelled breechclout)—a garment worn by Indian men; usually made from a long piece of soft deerskin, worn between the legs and held up in the front and back with a narrow belt.

dip nets—fishing nets used to scoop fish out of rushing water. Woven mesh is made by peeling fibers from the inner bark of elm or spruce trees, twisting the fibers into cord, and then weaving the cord into a net. The net is attached to a curved stick frame.

fishing weir—a woven structure made of wood and reeds that is placed in a river to catch fish.

Gluskabe (gloos-KAH-bee)—alternate spellings include Glooscap, Gluscap, Glooskabi. Mythological folk hero of Abenaki stories.

Great Illness—deadly epidemic (possibly typhoid fever, viral hepatitis, smallpox, plague, or chicken pox) that killed 95 percent of the Indian population between 1616 and 1619.

groundnuts—a climbing vine found in New England that has clusters of brown, fragrant flowers and small, edible tubers.

Kennebec—an Indian tribe that resided mostly in northern New Hampshire and Maine.

kettle hole—a round hollow in the ground that forms when a mass of buried ice melts.

King Philip—English name given to the Wampanoag leader known by Indians as Metacom.

King Philip's War—a series of violent raids and battles between Indians and colonists that raged throughout the towns and villages of New England from 1675 to 1676. Led by Wampanoag sachem Metacom (also known as King Philip).

King's Broad Arrow—three deep gashes cut into the tallest trees in the forest, reserving them for use as masts by the king of England.

Lamprey River—known by Indians as the Piscassic River "to the place of the little dark river."

lichen (LIKE-in)—a growing organism made up of fungi that partners with algae to create a crusty, scaly growth on tree trunks and rock.

lodge—similar to a wigwam; sometimes larger and built in an oval or rectangular shape.

maize—corn.

mast—a very strong, tall pole that holds the sails of a sailing ship.

Metacom—name of the Wampanoag chief also known as King Philip.

midden—a garbage dump, often excavated by archeologists to discover more about past cultures.

miller—a person who operates a mill, such as a sawmill (to cut lumber) or a grist mill (to grind grain into meal).

Moharimet (mo-HAHR-i-met)—the Abenaki sachem who lived in and ruled over the area now known as Dover, New Hampshire.

mudflats—flat, muddy, or sandy coastal area exposed when the tide goes out.

Newichawannok Trail—"place of extended rapids, at the fork," a trail that extended from as far north as Lake Ossipee, New Hampshire to South Berwick, Maine.

Ossipee Mountains—part of the White Mountains near the eastern border of New Hampshire.

Oyster River—original name for Durham, New Hampshire.

pelt—an animal skin with the fur still on it.

pemmican—a mix of powdered dried meat, berries, and animal fat hardened into a long-lasting, rich food.

Pentucket Trail—a trail that ran from Pentucket (now Haverhill, Massachusetts) through Cocheco (Dover, New Hampshire) to Quak (York, Maine).

pestle—a heavy stone tool, usually used with a stone or wooden mortar to grind grain, seeds, and other substances into meal or powder.

Piscataqua (pis-CA-tah-kwa)—Indian name for Portsmouth, New Hampshire (previously Strawbery Banke).

Piscataqua River—a river that runs through Portsmouth, New Hampshire.

Pond of Turtles—Turtle Pond in Lee, New Hampshire.

Portsmouth—New Hampshire seacoast town known as Strawbery Banke until 1653. Known as Piscataqua by Abenaki.

powwaw, paw-wau, powwow—Indian medicine man or medicine woman; sorcerer; shaman. Early settlers who watched powwaws heal the sick misunderstood the ceremonies and assumed that the word "powwow" described the ceremonial gathering of people, rather than the individual healer.

roe—fish eggs.

sachem (SA-chem)—Abenaki chief or leader.

sagamore—Abenaki chief or leader.

sawmill—a large mill and machine for sawing logs into boards.

schist—a metamorphic, crystalline rock found, among other places, in the White Mountains of New Hampshire.

shaman—magician, sorcerer, one who contacts the spirit world.

sinew—the tough tendon of an animal, used for rope or cord.

spawn—to deposit eggs for producing young, especially in large numbers.

sturgeon—a type of large fish that lives in the ocean but swims upstream in rivers to lay eggs.

talons—the sharp claws of an animal, especially a bird.

tipi (TEE-pee)—a type of shelter made by some Indian tribes, shaped like an inverted cone, often easy to put up, take down, and carry.

Wampanoag—an Indian tribe that resided mostly in Massachusetts and Rhode Island.

wampum—shell beads used for trade and money by both Indians and colonists, and for decoration and jewelry.

Washucke (wah-SHOOK-eh)—Abenaki word meaning "place on the hill," ancient Indian village at Wadleigh Falls now known as Woodchuck Hill. Also a clan name for one of the many bands of Abenaki Indians who call themselves the Only People. The Washucke were part of a loose alliance of thirteen Abenaki communities spread throughout New England and into Canada.

weir—*see* fishing weir.

Wheelwright—In 1638, Exeter, New Hampshire, was founded by Reverend John Wheelwright, a minister who had left the Massachusetts Bay Colony after religious conflict with the Puritan Church.

Wheelwright's Pond—In 1629, in hopes of maintaining peaceful relations, the sagamore (chief), Passaconaway, signed over vast amounts of land to the Reverend John Wheelwright, reserving the Indians' right to fish and hunt on that land.

White Mountains—a mountain range in northern New Hampshire.

wigwam—sturdy yet portable structure built for shelter by some tribes of Woodland Indians. The outer coverings (birch bark during cold weather; cattail mats during the summer) were windproof, waterproof, and could be rolled up and carried to a new campsite to cover different wigwams.

REFERENCES

Baier, Ursula, ed. *Lee in Four Centuries*. Lee, New Hampshire, 1966. **(Recommended resource book.)**

Berrill, Michael and Deborah Berrill. *Sierra Club Naturalist's Guide: The North Atlantic Coast*. San Francisco: Sierra Club Books, 1981.

Bragdon, Kathleen. *Native People of Southern New England, 1500-1650*. Norman, OK: University of Oklahoma Press, 1996.

Brockman, C. Frank. *Trees of North America: A Guide to Field Identification*. New York: Western Publishing Company, 1968.

Brooks, Laura. "Native American Political Issues: The People of the Dawnland." www.geocities.com/CapitolHill/9118/history1.html, Orono, ME: University of Maine, 1995.

Bruchac, Joseph. *Dog People: Native Dog Stories*. Golden, CO: Fulcrum Publishers, September 1995. **(Excellent for young readers.)**

Caduto, Michael J. *A Time Before New Hampshire: The Story of a Land and Native Peoples*. Lebanon, ME: University Press of New England, 2003. **(Recommended resource book.)**

Calloway, Colin G. "Abenaki." *Encyclopedia of North American Indians*, Frederick E. Hoxie, ed. New York: Houghton Mifflin Company, 1996. http://college.hmco.com/history/readerscomp/naind/html/na_000200_abenaki.html

"Canoe Building." www.greatdreams.com/canoe2.html

Cowasuck Band of the Pennacook-Abenaki People. "Abenaki Constitutional Convention." Draft 2. Revised July 1, 2002. http://www.cowasuck.org/constitution/

"Gershom Flagg: Descendants of Thomas French of Ipswich, MA, and others." http://worldconnect.rootsweb/com in www.RootsWeb.com

Harrison, Wade. "The King's Broad Arrow." Finnish Forest Research Institute (Metla) newsgroup submission. www.metla.fi/archive/forest/1995/06/msg00003.html, (1995).

Hoornbeek, Billee. "An Investigation into the Cause of Causes of the Epidemic Which Decimated the Indian Population of New England, 1616-1619." *The Indian Heritage of New Hampshire and Northern New England*, ed. Thaddeus Piotrowski. Jefferson, NC: McFarland & Company, Inc., 2002: 49-57.

"How the Dogs Became Companions to the People." From "Curriculum Based Activity for *Dog People*," www.fulcrum-resources.com/html/dog_people_exc.html Based on *Dog People: Native Dog Stories*. Joseph Bruchac and Murv Jacob (illus.). Golden, CO: Fulcrum Publishers, September 1995.

Manning, Samuel F. *New England Masts and the King's Broad Arrow*. Gardiner, ME: Tilbury House, 2000.

Marshall, Harlan A., comp. "The Manners, Customs, and Some Historical Facts About the Indians of Northern New England (Excerpts from Explorers and Missionaries, 1524-1657)." *The Indian Heritage of New Hampshire and Northern New England*, ed. Thaddeus Piotrowski. Jefferson, NC: McFarland & Company, Inc., 2002: 58-79. **(Recommended resource book.)**

McAdow, Ron. "Gluskabe." (1996). In "Abenaki Lifestyle and Tradition." www.native-languages.org/abenaki.html

Ndakinna Wilderness Project. "Characters from Western Abenaki Mythology."

Piotrowski, Thaddeus. "Indian Names in New Hampshire." *The Indian Heritage of New Hampshire and Northern New England*, ed. Thaddeus Piotrowski. Jefferson, NC: McFarland & Company, Inc., 2002: 178-92.

Piotrowski, Thaddeus. "Introduction: The Northeast." *The Indian Heritage of New Hampshire and Northern New England*, ed. Thaddeus Piotrowski. Jefferson, NC: McFarland & Company, Inc., 2002: 1-19.

Price, Chester. "Ancient Indian Places." *The Indian Heritage of New Hampshire and Northern New England*, ed. Thaddeus Piotrowski. Jefferson, NC: McFarland & Company, Inc., 2002: 175-77.

Price, Chester. "Historical Indian Trails of New Hampshire." *The Indian Heritage of New Hampshire and Northern New England*, ed. Thaddeus Piotrowski. Jefferson, NC: McFarland & Company, Inc., 2002: 154-74.

Reynolds, Cuyler, ed. *Hudson-Mohawk Genealogical and Family Memoirs*. Vol. 1, pp. 367-374. New York: Lewis Historical Publishing Company, 1911. http://www.schenectadyhistory.org/families/hmgfm/hilton-1.html

Russell, Howard S. *Indian New England Before the Mayflower*. Hanover, NH: University Press of New England, 1980.

Scales, John. *Colonial Era History of Dover, New Hampshire*. Bowie, MD: Heritage Books, Inc., 1977.

Scott, Rosemary. Personal conversation. Lee, NH, October 5, 2003.

Seymour, Tom. *Foraging New England*, Guilford, CT: The Globe Pequot Press, 2002. **(Excellent guide to medicinal and edible plants.)**

Sultzman, Lee. "Abenaki History." 1997. http://www.tolatsga.org/aben.html

Thompson, Mary P. *Landmarks in Ancient Dover, New Hampshire.* Durham, NH: Durham Historic Association, 1965.

Wolfson, Evelyn. *From Abenaki to Zuni.* New York: Walker and Company, 1988.

Yue, Charlotte and David. *The Wigwam and the Longhouse.* Boston: Houghton Mifflin Company, 2000. **(Excellent for young readers.)**

TIMELINE

1500s	Abenaki first encounter European influence
1564–1570	First major epidemic among native tribes
1586	Second major epidemic (typhus)
1617–1619	Third major epidemic (possibly chickenpox) leads to massive decimation.Up to ninety-five percent of the native population dies of disease.
1630	Strawbery Banke founded by Captain Walter Neal
1630s	Smallpox further decimates tribes
1640	Approximately 170 people living and working at Strawbery Banke, Isles of Shoals, and up Piscataqua River
1653	Strawbery Banke changes name to Portsmouth
1659	Wadononamin, sagamore of Washucke, sells Washucke and all land between Lamprey and Bellamy rivers to the English
1664	Robert Wadleigh starts construction of sawmill on Lamprey River
1668	Wadleigh Falls land is deeded to Robert Wadleigh by Dover, New Hampshire
1670	Abenaki form confederacy to fight the Iroquois and English

1675–1676	King Philip's War
1682	***The Story of Peter Little Bear* takes place (Peter Little Bear and Eben are eight to nine years old.)**
1685	Abenaki abandon permanent village at Wadleigh Falls
1688	A series of French and Indian Wars begins
July 6, 1690	**Battle at Wheelwright's Pond (Peter Little Bear and Eben are sixteen to seventeen years old)**
1695	Construction of Sherburne House in Portsmouth
1700	**Story ends (Peter Little Bear and Eben are about twenty-six years old)**
1969	**Lloyd Stevens discovers stone pestle in Lee, New Hampshire**

IDEAS TO THINK ABOUT

1. When does this story take place? What else was happening in our country at that time? What was happening in other parts of the world?

2. What is the life cycle of salmon and shad? Where do they live most of the year and why do they swim upstream in the spring and summer? What is roe? What does it mean to spawn?

3. How do you think the Lamprey River got its name? Where do other river names come from?

4. Make a list of all the Indian names you can think of in your area: rivers, street names, business names, school names, etc.

5. Look at the map of Lee, New Hampshire at the beginning of this book to see where the pestle was found. Can you find the Lamprey River on the map? Can you find Wadleigh Falls? Where was the Washucke camp located? Can you find Turtle Pond? Wheelwright Pond?

6. Visit the Lee, New Hampshire area and find some of the places mentioned in the story: Wadleigh Falls, Peter's Oven, Wheelwright's Pond, the Great Bay.

7. Visit the Great Bay at low tide and see what you find. Look for mussels, oysters, horseshoe crabs, lobsters, seals, blue herons, and bald eagles. Why do you think some of these animals are missing? What happened to them?

8. Think up your own Gluskabe story to explain how something came to be the way it is now.

9. There are many different ways to spell and pronounce Gluskabe. Glooscap, Gluscap, and Gluskabi are just a few. Why do you think this is? Why did the early settlers have trouble spelling Indian names? In modern times, why do our history books have trouble spelling Indian names?

10. If you were to choose an Indian name for yourself, what would it be? Choose a name that describes you in a special way. Think of names for your family members or friends.

11. Remember when Peter Little Bear and Eben threw the oyster and clam shells onto the pile of garbage at the Great Bay? That pile of shells is what archeologists call a **midden**. Talk about archeology and what scientists can learn from middens. What can we learn from the things people throw away? What will people in the future think about us by looking at our garbage?

12. Visit the Lee Historical Society in Lee, New Hampshire to see the pestle, arrowheads, and other Indian artifacts. Does the pestle look the way you expected it to? Visit your own local historical society or museum and ask about Indian artifacts.

About the Authors

A longtime resident of Lee, New Hampshire, and chair of the town's Conservation Commission for eighteen years, David Allan had a strong interest in the town's history as well. He served as president of the Lee Historical Society, designed its logo, and researched and wrote a history of the Lee Church. Allan collected legends and stories of early days in Lee and wrote the original story for this book.

Leslie Hamilton is author of the *Child's Play* series of craft and activities books for children. She is a freelance writer and editor and has lived in Lee, New Hampshire, for twenty-seven years.

Amy Daskal is a part-time artist who lives in Lee, New Hampshire, where she hosts creative workshops and helps to manage her family's commercial greenhouse.